Because I Could Not Stop My Bike

and Other Poems

Karen Jo Shapiro • Illustrated by Matt Faulkner

Whispering Coyote
A Charlesbridge Imprint

To my sweet daughter, Elina
—K. J. S.

For Mom and Dad—
You gave me the tools . . . I got busy.
Thank you.
—M. F.

Published by Charlesbridge
85 Main Street
Watertown, MA 02472
(617) 926-0329
www.charlesbridge.com

Library of Congress Cataloging-in-Publication Data
Shapiro, Karen Jo Giammusso, 1964–
   Because I could not stop my bike—and other poems/
   Karen Jo Giammusso Shapiro; illustrated by Matt Faulkner.
     p. cm.
   Summary: A collection of lighthearted parodies written
in the style of such well-known poets as Emily Dickinson,
Robert Burns, Christina Rossetti, Joyce Kilmer, and
William Shakespeare.
   ISBN 1-58089-035-0 (reinforced for library use)
   1. Children's poetry, American. [1. American poetry.
   2. Humorous poetry.] I. Faulkner, Matt, ill. II. Title.
   PS3619.H356B43   2003
   811'.54—dc21   2002010448

Manufactured in Singapore
(hc) 10 9 8 7 6 5 4 3 2 1

Illustrations done in watercolor and pen and ink on
   Arches 90 pound cold press watercolor paper
Display type and text type set in Woodrow and Calisto
Color separations, printing, and binding by Imago
Production supervision by Brian G. Walker
Designed by Diane M. Earley

"Do not ask for whom the poems are told.
The poems are told for you."

(with apologies to John Donne)

CONTENTS

Bark, Bark

With apologies to William Shakespeare (Cymbeline, *Act II, Scene iii*)

Bark, Bark! It's dark!
I wake before it's dawn,
while all the people in this house
sleep on and on and on.
I don't know why they sleep so long—
I sing a little doggie song:
"Bark, Bark. The park. Please walk me in the park."
I lick their feet and jump on beds.
I nuzzle up beside their heads.
And when they open up their eyes,
I bark, "Get up! It's time to rise!"

To My Dawdling Daughter

With apologies to Andrew Marvell ("To His Coy Mistress")

If in the morning we had time,
this dawdling, dear, would be no crime.
We could slow down and think which way
to get you ready for the day.

We'd take an hour to comb your hair,
two hours to choose the clothes you'd wear,
a half a day to tie your shoes,
to find the hat you always lose,
another day to wash your face;
well, dear, we'd do it at that pace.

But when I check the clock, I see
that time's sped by and we must flee.
Now let's get ready while we may—
we'll later have a chance to play.
These dawdling tricks will have to wait.
We're leaving now—let's not be late!

5

Dressing

With apologies to Alfred Tennyson ("In Memoriam, CVI")

Take off the Old, put on the New;
to get yourself dressed, that's all that you do.
Off with the Dirty, on with the Clean;
try it yourself—you'll see what I mean.
Toss yesterday's clothes—find the ones for today.
You got yourself dressed! Now let's go and play!

Mismatched Socks

With apologies to Robert Herrick ("Whenas in Silks my Julia Goes")

In mismatched socks my daughter goes.
Sometimes purple with red—who knows?
At least they cover up her toes!

Today I saw my daughter sweet,
with green and blue upon her feet—
and you know what? She sure looked neat!

Me

With apologies to Joyce Kilmer ("Trees")

I think that I will never see,
another person just like me.

Someone who has my color hair,
and picks the kind of clothes I wear.

Someone who thinks the thoughts I think,
and drinks the drinks I like to drink.

Who walks and talks my special way,
and plays the games I choose to play.

So many kinds of folks I see,
but only I can be a ME.

Where My Feet Go

*With apologies to William Shakespeare (*The Tempest*, Act V, Scene i)*

Where my feet go, there goes me.
But one day we did not agree.
I thought we'd go to the library,
but my feet wanted to climb a tree.

"Dear feet," I said, "oh, please be fair."
My feet said they'd be glad to share.
So now we all go EVERYWHERE.

9

Because I Could Not Stop My Bike

With apologies to Emily Dickinson ("Because I Could Not Stop For Death")

Because I could not stop my bike
it kindly stopped for me.
Unluckily, it did not stop
until it hit a tree.

How fast we rode; at what a speed
I pedaled down the hill!
I did not know the brakes were stuck
until I took that spill.

I must admit, it was a thrill
to feel so fast and free—
I think we would be whizzing still
if we'd not hit that tree!

How Do I Love Ketchup? Let Me Count the Ways

With apologies to Elizabeth Barrett Browning ("How Do I Love Thee?")

How do I love ketchup? Let me count the ways . . .
I tried it first on burgers and fries,
that's all I did for many days,
until I bought more, in a larger size.

I tried it on my eggs and toast;
spaghetti, too, sure tasted nice!
I like the ketchup part the most.
I love it on my beans and rice.

I add it to all my soups and stews;
On vegetables a little spurt;
a dash on fruit, and if I choose—
I'll even have it on dessert.

I Eat My Pickle

With apologies to Edna St. Vincent Millay ("First Fig")

I eat my pickle from both ends.
It will not last the night.
But, oh my family and my friends—
I really love each bite!

The Generous Boy to His Friend

With apologies to Christopher Marlowe ("The Passionate Shepherd to His Love")

Come sit with me and share my lunch.
I have some vegetables to munch—
tomatoes, carrots, celery, too—
peas that you can shell and chew.
I have apples ripe and red,
peanut butter, oatmeal bread.
I have a chunk of cheddar cheese;
all the juice that you could please,
lemon yogurt in a dish,
whole wheat crackers if you wish—
grapes and cherries by the bunch.
Won't you come and share my lunch?

Her Reply

With apologies to Sir Walter Raleigh ("The Nymph's Reply")

If cookies were in front of you—
Doughnuts, candy, ice cream, too—
If you had pretzels there to munch,
I'd sit with you and share your lunch.

I eat cupcakes frosted pink.
Chocolate milk is what I drink.
Although I'd like your company,
I don't like food that's good for me!

But give me soda with some ice,
greasy pizza by the slice,
potato chips so nice to crunch—
Then I would sit and share your lunch!

A Messy Room

With apologies to William Blake ("A Poison Tree")

I made a mess.
I let it go.
I used more toys.
The mess did grow.

I lost some crayons.
I spilled some glue.
I pulled out books.
The clutter grew.

And every time
that I would play
I did not put
my things away.

Soon stuff covered
all the floor.
"That's what," I said,
"the floors are for."

Junk all around,
Mess on each shelf.
Till the day I could not
find myself!

Where Is Your Pail, Sand-Scooper?

With apologies to Sir John Suckling ("Why So Pale and Wan")

Where is your pail, Sand-Scooper?
Where is your pail, my friend?
You have a blue shovel and that's really super!
But where can you put the sand in the end—
if you have no pail, my friend?

A Red, Red Nose

With apologies to Robert Burns ("A Red, Red Rose")

Oh! My nose is like a red, red rose
That's newly burnt in June.
Oh! My nose was in the hot, hot sun
All yesterday afternoon.

Burnt as you are, my little nose,
Yet redder is each ear;
And I shall peel until I heal—
A week or two, I fear.

Next time we're at the beach, dear nose,
Where children play and run,
We'll be the one with the big white hat,
Under the hot, hot sun.

19

The Constant Shirt-Wearer

With apologies to Sir John Suckling ("The Constant Lover")

On with it! I've worn this shirt
for three whole days together,
and I will wear it for three more,
in rain or sunny weather.

I put it on, I do not care
if it has lots of dirt.
For I have never loved my clothes,
the way I love this shirt.

I Never Saw a Talking Hat

With apologies to Emily Dickinson ("I Never Saw a Moor")

I never saw a talking hat
or elf of any kind.
But one day I imagined them—
I saw them in my mind.

A lion that loves lemonade,
a chunk of chocolate cheese—
with my imagination,
I can think up what I please!

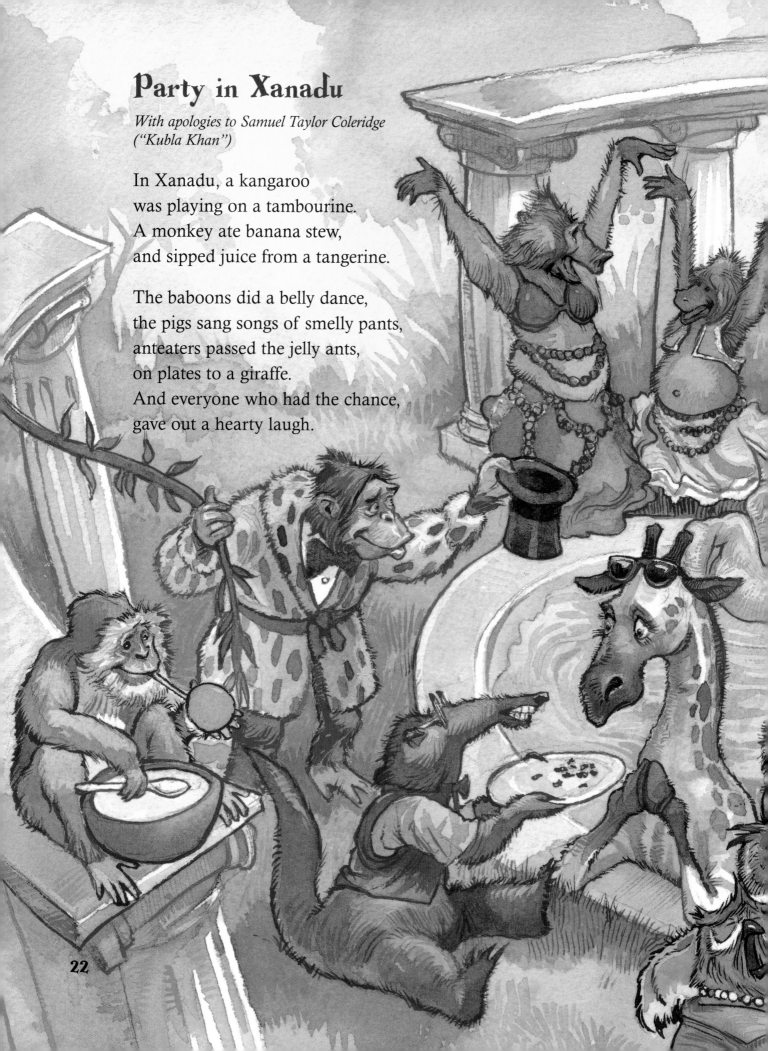

Party in Xanadu

*With apologies to Samuel Taylor Coleridge
("Kubla Khan")*

In Xanadu, a kangaroo
was playing on a tambourine.
A monkey ate banana stew,
and sipped juice from a tangerine.

The baboons did a belly dance,
the pigs sang songs of smelly pants,
anteaters passed the jelly ants,
on plates to a giraffe.
And everyone who had the chance,
gave out a hearty laugh.

The zebras played a pair of flutes,
the frogs sky-dived with parachutes,
the chimps arrived in hairy suits,
and nobody was bored.
The owls filled the air with hoots,
and how the lion roared!

Oh, such a party you won't find,
in circus or in zoo.
But if you want a grand old time,
hop down to Xanadu!

My Birthday

With apologies to Christina Rossetti ("A Birthday")

My heart is like a flying bird,
that sings a silly tune.
My heart is like a rocket ship,
that rushes to the moon.
My heart is like a big parade,
where horns and trumpets play.
My heart is gladder than all these—
My birthday is today!

Make me a yummy chocolate cake—
with fancy frosting too.
Wrap me a present in silver and red—
a special one from you.
Sing me the "Happy Birthday" song,
and I will clap with glee—
For everyone can see I am
a one-year-older me!

24

Oh, Mommy! My Mommy!

With apologies to Walt Whitman ("O Captain! My Captain!")

"Oh, Mommy! My Mommy! Tell me, please, are we there yet?
From what you said the last time, the answer's 'NO,' I'll bet.
I'm tired of just sitting still, I'm tired of this car.
I'm tired of you turning on that show called NPR.
I have to go potty and my seatbelt's hurting, too.
I've used up all my games and books. I have a dismal view.
Oh! Back here there is nothing to do! do! do!"

In front my mother's driving, did she not hear me somehow?
So I say a little louder, "Are we there yet, Mommy, NOW?"

Macaroni and Cheese

With apologies to Edgar Allen Poe ("Annabel Lee")

It was many and many a week ago
that I and my sister Louise
first tried out a food that you might know
called macaroni and cheese.

Now I was so hungry and she was so hungry
we ate it as fast as you please.
When we emptied our plates, we said, "BOY, THAT WAS GREAT!"
"LET'S HAVE MORE MACARONI AND CHEESE!"
We had seconds and thirds and we thought about fourths—
but it would have been too tight a squeeze.

When we were quite small, there was many a fight
between myself and Louise,
But on that fine day we knew we'd unite
over macaroni and cheese.
When I said gaily, "Let's have this food daily,"
my sister replied, "I agree."

Now the moon never beams without bringing us dreams
of macaroni and cheese,
and the stars never rise but you'll hear our loud cries
for macaroni and cheese.

And every noon, we sing a bright tune,
for we know we'll be eating it soon.
No matter how others will marvel or tease,
we eat macaroni and cheese.

Fancy Bread

With apologies to William Shakespeare
(The Merchant of Venice, *Act III, Scene ii*)

Do you want some fancy bread?
With jam and butter it is spread,
and you could bring a slice to bed.
Reply, reply.

Yes, I'd like your fancy bread,
but in the dining room instead.
I don't want bread crumbs in the bed.
That's why, that's why.

The Tiger

With apologies to William Blake ("The Tiger")

Tiger, Tiger took a bite
out of my dessert last night.
That chocolate cake was mine, you know—
But I did not dare tell him so.

Why did I let him eat my cake?
When I got near, my hands would shake.
I feared if I said "NO," you see,
that he would take a bite of me!

Tiger, Tiger saw my plight
and said, "I'm sorry for last night.
I did not know it was your cake—
next time I'll ask before I take."

Our Breath

With apologies to William Shakespeare (As You Like It, Act II, Scene vii)

Blow, Blow, on hot soup blow.
Our breath's a funny tool.
It warms up chilly hands,
but makes our hot food cool.

The Toddler

With apologies to Alfred Tennyson ("The Eagle")

He grabs a chair with little hands
and pulls and tugs until he stands.
He's setting off for distant lands!

Most of the time my brother crawls.
Today he's clinging onto walls.
He takes a step, but—OOPS!—he falls!

Sing Me a Song, My Daddy

With apologies to Christina Rossetti ("Song")

When I am giggling and skipping about,
Sing a GLAD song for me.
And if I am stomping and starting to shout,
Sing a MAD song for me.
And when I am crying or wearing a pout,
Sing a SAD song for me.

When I am afraid, a SCARED song is nice.
If I'm REALLY afraid, would you please sing it twice?

A song for the morning
To wake up brand-new . . .
And when I am sleepy
A NIGHT song will do!

31

We Outgrow Shoes Like Other Things

With apologies to Emily Dickinson ("We Outgrow Love Like Other Things")

We outgrow shoes, like other things,
and put them in a drawer,
'til one day we cannot believe
what tiny shoes we wore!